FRANKENSTEIN'S FRIGHT BEFORE CHRISTMAS

story & pictures by

Ludworst Bemonster

FEIWEL AND FRIENDS · NEW YORK

DEADICATIONS

To Patrick and Marquie,
a frightfully fine family.
—R. W.

To Scarlett and Wren,
cute little monsters.
—N. H.

A FEIWEL AND FRIENDS BOOK
An Imprint of Macmillan

FRANKENSTEIN'S FRIGHT BEFORE CHRISTMAS.
Text copyright © 2014 by Rick Walton.
Illustrations copyright © 2014 by Nathan Hale.
Printed in China by Toppan Leefung Printing Ltd., Dongguan City, Guangdong Province.
For information, address Feiwel and Friends, 175 Fifth Avenue, New York, N.Y. 10010.
Feiwel and Friends books may be purchased for business or promotional use. For information on
bulk purchases, please contact the Macmillan Corporate and Premium Sales Department
at (800) 221-7945 x5422 or by e-mail at specialmarkets@macmillan.com.

Library of Congress Cataloging-in-Publication Data is available

ISBN 978-0-312-55367-8

The artwork was created with Kuretake brush pens and Rapidograph Ultradraw ink.
It was colored with M. Graham Watercolors and Photoshop.

Feiwel and Friends logo designed by Filomena Tuosto

First Edition: 2014

1 3 5 7 9 10 8 6 4 2

mackids.com

'Twas the night before Christmas and poor Miss Devel
was hassled and harried, and not feeling well.
The monsters' bad manners had taken their toll.
They'd lost their heads! They were out of control!

Then finally, the monsters
bonked their heads,
pulled out their teeth,
and wet their beds.

At last, Miss Devel
sighed with relief
and climbed into bed—
but her rest would be brief.

For off in the distance, she heard such a clatter.

She sprang from her slab to see what was the matter.

Off down the stairs, she flew like a flash,
and threw open the doors just in time for the

CRASH!

"Now what's going on here?" she yelled.

"Tell me quick!"

Frankenstein said,

"It's a tree for Saint Nick!

He's coming tonight!

He has presents! That's why . . ."

But a voice interrupted,

from somewhere up high . . .

"On Whoozit, on Whatzit, and all of you others.

Our next stop—some kids with no fathers or mothers!

These poor, sweet young children need extra good cheer.

For them, we have brought special presents this year!"

Then creaking and cracking from up on the roof.
And next through the ceiling, a small reindeer hoof.

One more, then another, poked into the room.
And down fell Saint Nick and his sleigh with a

BOOM!

The sack opened wide.
It could no longer hold
gifts hidden inside.
So out the gifts rolled.

"New heads!" yelled the
monsters, and all piled on.
In seconds, the gifts (and Saint
Nick) were all gone.

Frankenstein stood
to the side by himself.
"My brother," he proudly
explained, "is Head Elf."

Eleven proud monsters
beamed with delight.
Until Miss Devel shouted,
"Something's not right!"

The mix-up was fixed up, and soon, all was fine.

And then they all noticed poor Frankenstein.

"There are presents for us, but no present for you!
You must have a gift. What can we do?"

The whole world went quiet. What would he say?
Frankenstein stared at the reindeer and sleigh.

And then he looked longingly up to the sky.

Then turned to Saint Nick and said,

"I want TO FLY!"

He jumped in the sleigh and he picked up a rein.

And before Miss Devel could protest or complain,

or explain that the monsters should be in their beds,
the sleigh filled with monsters with happy new heads.

"Come too, Miss Devel! There is room here for one."
"No, thank you. I'm good. You be safe and have fun."

And she smiled and said as they soared out of sight,

"Happy Christmas to me!

To you monsters, good night!"